SISTERS FOREVER

Adapted by Lexi Ryals

Based on the series created by John D. Beck & Ron Hart

Part One is based on the episode "Twinsconsin," written by John D. Beck & Ron Hart

Part Two is based on the episode "Team-A-Rooney," written by John D. Beck & Ron Hart

DISNEP PRESS

Los Angeles • New York

Printed in the United States of America
First Edition, January 2015
3 5 7 9 10 8 6 4 2
V475-2873-0-14363

Library of Congress Control Number: 2014951111
ISBN 978-1-4847-1079-1

For more Disney Press fun, visit www.disneybooks.com
Visit DisneyChannel.com

SUSTAINABLE
FORESTRY
INITIATIVE

Certified Chain of Custody
Promoting Sustainable Forestry

www.sfiprogram.org
SFI-01054

The SFI label applies to the text stock

Sophie Treanor

SISTERS FOREVER

PART

ONE

Maddie

I can't believe it. Today is finally the day—the day my identical twin sister, Liv, comes home for good. That sounds dramatic, huh? Well, let me explain. My name is Maddie Rooney. I'm fifteen years old and I live in Wisconsin. My sister, Liv, moved to Hollywood to live with our aunt a few years ago when she was cast as the lead actress on the hottest musical TV show ever. It's called *Sing It Loud!* Ever heard of it? Of course you have. Anyway, *Sing It Loud!* just came to an end after four long years. Liv probably could have stayed in Hollywood and landed a spot on a new TV show, but she decided to come home instead and finish high school with me. *Bam!* What?!

So, like I said, she's coming home today and I'm excited and nervous and I can't wait. I cleaned our room, made sure she has plenty of space in our closet, and even planned the most perfectly Liv-esque surprise welcome-back party. I decorated the living room with really cool pink and purple balloons shaped like hearts, because if there's anything Liv loves more than balloons, it's hearts and stars. I just want everything to be perfect.

All that's left is hanging up the WELCOME HOME banner I made. Dad's helping me hang it, since he's so tall. But, um, he's not doing the best job. Time to step in.

"No, Dad, no. Okay, it needs to go up. More. More. Up more. Down a tiny bit." When the banner's finally level, I say, "Perfect! Twin sister officially welcomed. *Bam!* What?!" (In case you haven't noticed, "*Bam!* What?!" is kind of my catchphrase.)

With the banner in place, the living room finally looks ready for Liv.

Time to make sure we have the snacks covered. You can't have a homecoming without snacks, right?

I spin around to face Mom, who is rearranging the balloons. "Okay, Mom, snack update. Where's Liv's favorite dip?"

"Oh, you mean *this* dip?" my younger brother Joey mumbles from where he's seated on the couch, his mouth full of vegan spinach-artichoke dip.

"We're going to need more," says my youngest brother, Parker, who's sitting next to Joey. He and Joey have nearly polished off all the dip, carrots, and cucumbers I set out five minutes ago. It's not a big deal. Actually, it's a big deal!

"You two are *eating the dip*?" I shout. "This is Wisconsin, you can't welcome people home without dip! You two are officially banned from the welcome-home zone!"

My brothers are the worst. They are just such annoying dweebs most of the time. Okay, that's not totally true. I mean, I love them, and I won't ever admit this to them, but they're both really smart in different ways. But right now, they're officially the worst.

"Maddie," Mom says sweetly, "if you're freaking out

about Liv coming home, we should talk." My mom is a psychologist, so she always wants to talk about feelings.

I take a deep breath and smile. "Mom, she's my twin, my built-in best friend," I assure her. "I'm not freaking out."

But of course I'm freaking out! Starting tomorrow, I'm going to high school with my celebrity sis. And we have the same face, yet *she's* the "cute one." I mean, what if everyone at school likes her better than me? What if Diggie, the guy I've been crushing on all year, decides he likes my sister instead of me? What if Liv and I don't get along anymore? There are a lot of "what ifs." I just have to keep breathing and remember I'm excited to see her. Everything's going to be fine.

"Hey, guys!" says Parker, pointing out the window. "A limo pulled up and there's a bunch of people with cameras on our lawn!" Parker jumps up and runs over to peer outside.

Joey nods. "Either Liv's home early or I won the zoo's name-the-baby-elephant contest."

Mom and Dad join Parker at the window, followed by Joey and me.

Well, here goes nothing.

Liv's back and nothing will ever be the same again.

Walking up to my house is absolutely the best feeling in the whole wide world! Well, next to giving makeovers to those in need. I pull my suitcases up onto the front porch. You'd think someone would have come out to help me by now. I mean, it's not like I've ever been known to travel light. I, Liv Rooney, star of *Sing It Loud!*, seriously own over one hundred pairs of fabulous shoes.

I just finished the final season of my smash-tastic TV show *Sing it Loud!* It was one of those super-realistic shows where kids would suddenly break into song for no reason. I loved Hollywood and I'd been offered a quazillion other shows and movies, but I missed my family—especially my twin and best friend, Maddie. It was time to come home. So here I am!

I turn and pose for the paparazzi waiting on my lawn, flashing them my trademark smile and waving. "I'll miss you, paparazzi," I say more to myself than to them. "When I walk through this door, I will be just another regular fifteen-year-old girl."

I try not to let them see how nervous I am. To tell you the truth, I am freaking out about how to become just a regular girl. I haven't gone to a regular school since fifth grade, and now I am a sophomore in high school. What if everything that was cool in Hollywood is totally different from what is cool in Wisconsin? What if no one likes me? What if Maddie and I don't get along anymore? Nope! Only positive thinking allowed. Everything will be amazing!

"Boom, boom, boom—send," I say brightly to the photographers, hitting three different poses. (That was my catchphrase on *Sing It Loud!*) I blow them a kiss and turn away from the flashing cameras to go into my house, but the door won't open.

I try it again and the door flies open. Before me, I see Maddie waiting for a hug.

I squeal. "You stole my face!"

"I had it first!" Maddie counters. We hug each other tightly.

We really couldn't be more different. I am wearing a black leather peplum top and sparkly leggings. My hair is down and curled, my makeup is obviously flawless, and I am carrying my favorite hot-pink handbag. Maddie, on the other hand, is wearing glasses, sweats, and a sports T-shirt. Her hair is in a ponytail and she wears no makeup at all. But none of those differences matter to me; Maddie will always be my best friend. I hug her again.

"Take notes," Parker says to Joey. "That's what it looks like when a girl is *happy* to see you."

"Thanks, Parker. And this is what it looks like inside my armpit," Joey says. He grabs Parker's face and buries it in his armpit.

I stroll over to my two younger brothers. "Aw, I was worried you two grew up while I was away," I say, and give each of them a hug. My brothers are totally immature dorks, but I've missed them.

"Yeah, there's no chance of that happening," Joey says, shaking his head.

"Um, the people who gave you *life* are still waiting for their hugs," Dad says.

"Oh, right, you guys," I joke, trotting over and hugging Mom and Dad.

I'm having trouble not tearing up. It's really good to be home. I take a step back from Mom and Dad. "Sorry about the camera-palooza," I say. "They're just here for my homecoming."

"Oh, who cares?" Mom says with a smile. "All my babies are under one roof!" She pulls out her phone. "Family photo time!" We all gather around her and she holds out her phone at arm's length to take a faboosh family selfie. I really hope she gets my good side. Who am I kidding? I only *have* good sides. Maddie is leaping up and down to get in the frame: we can't all fit.

I have the best idea. I tap Mom's shoulder. "Mom," I say. "I've got this!"

A few seconds later we are all on the front porch. Luckily, the paparazzi are still there. I stand back and study my family. "Okay, people, say 'dazzleberry'!" I tell them in my signature singsongy voice. I step in beside Maddie, throw my arm up, kick up one heel, and give the cameras my best red-carpet smile.

"Dazzleberry!" my family says in unison.

Then a host of flashbulbs go off.

Sometimes being famous can really come in handy!

I **spend the whole evening** helping Liv unpack.
If it had been me moving home, we'd mainly be
throwing a bag's worth of gym clothes into the dresser
and hanging up one or two shirts, but Liv's unpacking
is a different story. We've been at it for hours—color
coordinating and sorting by season, pattern, and
length.

Liv and I have always shared a room, and it's going
to be nice actually having her occupying her side of
the room again. My half features a plain desk, a big
bed with a basketball headboard, ribbons and trophies
hanging from the wall, and shelves racked with sports

gear. Liv's half of the room has a turquoise velvet bench, several mirrors, lots of scarves and necklaces hanging from wall hooks, and a bed with a glittery white headboard.

I plop down at my desk, pick up my spare pair of glasses, and turn to Liv. "Okay, returning fashionista," I say, holding up both pairs of glasses to my face, "which glasses should I go with—green or purple?"

Liv drops the blouse she was folding and trots over to me.

"If I were you, I'd go with contacts and a little mascara," Liv says with a smile. I laugh. She knows I'm not a contacts-and-mascara-wearing girl. I hate having anything touch my eyes—and I only use mascara when I absolutely have to. It's so nice to have Liv home. She knows me better than anyone else on Earth.

I put down the spare pair and look at Liv. "How *great* is this? Liv and Maddie, back in the same room together," I say, smiling. "Oh! I got you a little welcome-home gift!" I lift up a special remote control that I made for her.

I press the button on the remote. "Ta-da!"

The poster above Liv's headboard lights up. It took me weeks to hook it up with all its tiny blinking lights. The flashy poster looks beautiful. It says "Sing It Loud!" in huge letters, along with other Liv-isms, like "Choose Happiness" and "Dreams Do Come True," written around it.

"O-M-Wowza!" Liv squeals, clapping her hands in delight.

"Go ahead," I say to her. "Take a diva moment."

Liv hops up on the bed and strikes a pose in front of the poster. Then she sings. She hits a note and holds it. My sis really does have a fantastic voice. I clap.

Just then Mom and Dad throw the door open and rush in.

"We heard a noise," Mom says, looking around frantically.

"Everything okay?" Dad asks.

Liv and I both look at them like they're crazy.

"We're fine," I tell them.

"Yeah," Liv says. "Just doing twin stuff."

"Well, your twin stuff can get a little intense," Mom says. "Don't forget about the curling iron incident of sixth grade."

"In *my* defense," I say, "who sneaks up behind someone and tries to *curl their hair*?"

Liv pushes her hair to the side and points at her forehead. "I have a *huge* scar. It's right here." She feels her forehead, searching for the non-existent scar. "Wait, it's here somewhere, I'll find it. It's horrible."

"But we're more mature now," I say. "No more twin drama."

"Right, no more twin drama," Liv says.

"I give it a day," Dad whispers to Mom. "They're a ticking time bomb."

"Shouldn't you be at one of your weird parental fun nights? Like square dancing or couples yoga?" I ask them as they walk out the door.

"Tell me you didn't sign us up for couples yoga," Dad says to Mom.

"It's on Wednesday. Don't wear your tights," Mom says as she pulls the door shut.

I roll my eyes and face Liv, turning my charm bracelet around and around on my wrist and trying not to blush. "I'm *so* glad you're home. There's something I've been *dying* to tell you about."

Liv gasps and jumps down from the bed. "This is about a boy!"

I stare at her in disbelief. "How'd you know that?"

"When you get nervous, you still play with the charm bracelet I gave you. Duh," Liv says, widening her eyes at me. "Now back to the boy: is he *cute*?"

"Are you *nosy* and *sparkly*?" I ask her sarcastically.

Liv squeals and claps. "Then he *is* cute! Spill." She sits back on the bed.

I laugh. It feels so good to talk to Liv. I've been dying to tell someone about my crush for *months*. "Well, his name is Diggie and he's captain of the basketball team. And you know that competitive thing I get where I grind my opponents into submission?" I sigh and smile. "He has it, too."

"Wow," Liv laughs. "Blush much? Someone has a serious case of the Diggies!"

"I do," I say. I can't stop smiling. "This is so great to talk about. I'm kind of hoping he asks me to the dance this weekend, and he hasn't exactly—"

"Ooh," Liv interrupts. "Speaking of dance, I've got

the series finale of *Sing it Loud!* Do you want to see a sneak peak?" She picks up her tablet, taps the screen a few times, and passes it to me.

I watch as Liv dances and sings on-screen. Her performance is amazing, as usual, with backup dancers, a cool outfit, and colorful stage lights. And the song is pretty catchy. But I can't focus on it too well. I can't figure out why she's showing it to me when I was in the middle of telling her about my crush. "Liv, this is great, but we were talking about Diggie," I say gently, setting down the tablet.

"Absolutely," she says, picking up the tablet. "But you haven't even seen the best part!" She hands the tablet back to me.

I watch Liv's song and dance routine until the music video ends.

"What'd you think?" she asks breathlessly, then squeals and stands up.

I can't believe she's being so rude. I've been waiting for weeks to tell her about Diggie, and I want her advice, but she's acting like it doesn't even matter. I guess I've been stupid to think she actually matured.

As usual, it's all Liv all the time. Maybe things won't be as good as I'd hoped after all. I hand her the tablet. "I think you cut me off when I was telling you about something really important to me," I say. "Liv, you're the first person I've even mentioned Diggie to."

"Well, Maddie, you're the first person I've shown *this* to," Liv says, hugging her tablet to her. Then she pauses. "Except for everybody on the plane. They all thought it was amazing." She smiles and laughs.

I put my hands on my hips. "You know what I thought was amazing?" I say. "I actually thought we were going to talk about *me* for once." I storm to the door. I need to clear my head. But I almost run right into Mom and Dad, who were waiting outside in the hall. They stumble past me and into the bedroom.

"We weren't listening," Dad says, blushing.

"Neither was she," I tell him, trying not to cry.

Mom stoops and picks up my curling iron. "You know, I'm just going to hold on to this curling iron for the next few years," she says.

Parker

I couldn't sleep, so I snuck down to the garage to play video games. The garage is full of old stuff, and me and Joey have always used it as a fun place to hang out.

Joey steps into the room. He's got a sandwich. "What are you doing out here in the garage? Do Mom and Dad know you're awake?" he asks me.

"Nope. They're too focused on Liv and Maddie to notice anything we're doing. I spent all afternoon on the roof with a homemade catapult blasting joggers with buckets of mashed potatoes," I say.

"Huh," Joey says. "You know, you're right. They didn't say a word when I made beans and didn't clean the pot." He pauses and looks sort of thoughtful. "The two of us are using our freedom a little differently." He shakes his head. Then he jumps up in excitement. "Wait. If we can get away with anything, we should team up—for something *big*."

Now he's talking. I think of all the cool things we could do.

"Take the car and drive to Vegas?" I ask, grinning.

"Smaller," Joey says. "Let's put this TV *in our room*."

"But Mom and Dad say we can't have a TV in our room." I slump back in my chair.

"Mom and Dad *who*?" Joey says. "So, what if our room wasn't our room? What if it was our . . . bro cave?"

Joey and his big ideas. "What's a bro cave?" I ask him.

"Forget this crummy garage. In a bro cave, we'd have everything we could possibly want in our room: a TV, food, a hot tub with a high dive, that invisible zebra you're always talking to," Joey explains.

I roll my eyes. "I was *four*. Let it go!" I say.

"Bro cave, bro," Joey says. "No parents, no twins,

just you and me blasting mutant video-game bunnies in our underwear. Close your eyes and let me take you there."

I close my eyes, and my face breaks into a big grin. I can see it now. A bro cave unlike any other, with good snacks and endless hours of playing wicked cool video games.

Joey smacks me on the forehead.

"Ah!" I shout.

"Ha!" Joey says. "Never gets old."

Joey

Me and Parker are sneaking through the living room. I'm carrying the TV from the garage—boy, this thing is heavy—and Parker is dragging a lightweight inflatable chair. Our bro cave is going to have all the fixings for the ultimate hangout spot. We're moving slowly and quietly, since Mom and Dad are watching a movie on the couch, eating popcorn from the family's old-timey popcorn machine. Hopefully they can't hear us over their crunching and munching. Parker and I creep behind them and freeze when they start talking.

"Is it just me or is Liv moving home going to be harder than we thought?" Mom asks Dad.

Dad puts his arm around Mom's shoulder. "It's not

going to be easy, but we'll make it work. We just have to have eyes in the back of our heads."

"You're right. Sure, there's four of them and we're outnumbered. But we're smarter than they are," Mom says pretty confidently.

"Unlike the Johnsons next door. I'm pretty sure it was their jerk kid, Ernie, who hit me with a glob of mashed potatoes earlier," Dad says, shaking his head.

Me and Parker exchange glances. I think we both know that Ernie isn't the culprit. I shift the TV under one arm and grab the popcorn machine with the other.

I nod for Parker to keep moving. We creep upstairs like ninjas.

Our bro cave is going to be so cool! Especially with the popcorn machine!

Today is my first day at a regular high school. Ever. I'm nervous, but I don't let it show. Of course, as soon as I arrived, I was swarmed by fans of my show, *Sing It Loud!* So I'm doing what any good star who wants to make friends would do: I'm posing for pictures and signing autographs. Then I remember what time it is. I only have five minutes to find my locker before the bell rings. Eek!

"Boom, boom, boom—send!" I say to the crowd of fans. "You guys are so sweet. Thank you so much." I spot Joey and hurry over to him. "I so wasn't expecting that," I say to him.

"Sorry no one's paying attention to you," Joey says sarcastically. "That must be hard."

"Okay, back your breath up." I hand him a mint. "Two questions: Where's Maddie's locker? And why is that hamster staring at me?" I point a perfectly manicured finger to a hideous giant gold statue covered in sausage links.

"It's not a hamster," Joey tells me defensively. "It's our school mascot, Paulie the Fighting Porcupine. On game days, jocks rub his tummy for luck and adorn him with bratwurst."

I scrunch up my nose. "I am soooo back in Wisconsin."

Just then Mom and Dad come walking down the hallway.

"Oh, no! Mom and Dad! Initiate turtle mode," Joey says frantically. He flips the hood of his sweatshirt up and pulls it shut so all I can see is his nose. My perfectly fashionable ensemble does not allow for that, so I hold up my gorgeous turquoise leather handbag to hide my face.

I mean, I knew that Dad coached the girls' basketball team and that Mom was the school psychologist, but knowing it and feeling the shame of them walking past me in the hall are two co

"Think we've embarrassed

says loudly.

"Not quite," Dad says, lool

Then he pulls Mom in for a

lips. I try not to scream. Ugh

"Don't look directly at them," Joey whispers to me, looking as horrified as I feel.

I spot Maddie at her locker down the hall and hurry over to her before Mom and Dad can do anything else. I tap her on the shoulder. She glares at me. Uh-oh.

"I'm sorry about last night," I say. I really do feel bad about it. I hate fighting with Maddie. "I wasn't trying to get you all grumple-stiltskin," I add.

Maddie's face softens. "It's cool. You were just excited to show me your video."

I let out the breath I didn't realize I was holding. Yay! Maddie and I are friends again. "I'm glad we're okay," I say. I smile and then pull out my phone. "Did you want to see it again?" I say, shaking my phone and laughing.

Maddie laughs, too, and says, "No."

here goes that idea!

handsome guy wearing a basketball letter walks over to us. "S'up, Rooney?" he says, king right at Maddie.

Maddie stops laughing and starts spinning her charm bracelet around her wrist. She has a really weird look on her face, and she leans back against her locker with her arms crossed over her chest. "S'up, Diggie?" she says in a trying-to-be-cool voice that I immediately know she uses just for him. She gives him a painfully tense smile. Honeybee needs to learn how to ease up!

"Ooh, so *this* is Diggie," I say, smiling, looking back and forth between them. It's no wonder she looks so nervous.

"Live and in person for your viewing pleasure!" Diggie says in a loud, booming voice, like one of those guys on ESPN. When he sees my confused expression, he switches back to his normal voice. "I want to be a sports announcer after I play pro ball, so I'm just practicing."

I clap my hands and squeal. "Fun! How would you introduce me?"

"Okay," Diggie says. Then he looks down and back up and booms, *"If you're seeing double, do not adjust your screens. It's the incomparable, the unstoppable, if she were popcorn, she'd be poppable, Liv Rrrrrooooney!"*

He is adorable, and *perfect* for Maddie. I elbow her and say, "Um, approved!"

"So, Rooney Classic," he says with his eyes on Maddie, "what are you doing later?"

"Um . . . stuff," Maddie says, trying to act nonchalant.

She should seriously leave the acting to me.

Diggie nods, a little disappointed. "Got it. Peace out, Rooneys!" He walks down the hall.

I turn to Maddie and throw up my hands. "'S'up'? 'Stuff'? That's how you *flirt*?"

"Liv, flirting's a game. If Diggie knows I like him, I lose the advantage. And if I lose the advantage, I lose. And I don't lose. *Bam!* What?!" Maddie says.

There she goes getting all "sports rage" on me.

But she has it all wrong. "Okay, stop with the sports nonsense and listen to me. If you want Diggie to ask you to the dance, you need *major* help," I tell her.

"No." Maddie shakes her head. "I do not need your

help getting Diggie. Do you hear me? Do not help."
She marches off to class.

But there is no way I'm not going to help her. After
our huge fight last night, I need to do something super
sweet and nice for her. Plus, I've never heard such a
clear cry for help. I mean, seriously? Besides, I know
just what to do. . . .

Eek! Well, look at the time! I am going to be so
late for class.

Since Maddie isn't planning to go back to her locker
anytime soon, I know I'm in the clear to put my plan
into motion. After class, I tie my hair in a ponytail,
slip on Maddie's spare pair of glasses (She must have
really bad vision; these things are intense!), and shrug
on her purple basketball jacket, which I found in
her locker. The jacket's actually kind of cute . . . in a
sporty jacket-y kind of way. Though it could use some
gemstones.

Joey walks over just as I am checking my hair in
Maddie's ridiculously tiny locker mirror. She needs a
full-length one stat! One with bright lights around it.

I try out my impression on Joey. "S'up, Joey? It's me, Maddie."

He doesn't even give me a second look. So I grab him and whisper, "It's not really Maddie. It's Liv!"

"Liv, what are you doing?" he says.

"I got off on the wrong foot with Maddie, but I'm going to fix that in a way that only an actress like me can. I'm going to land her a date to the dance!" I say.

"Man, I wish I had a twin brother that would help me land a date to the dance," Joey says as he walks off, right past Diggie. "I would call him Michael."

"Yo, Diggie. S'up?" I say in my best Maddie voice.

"S'up, Rooney?" he says with a smile.

"Stuff. So, what do you say, you, me, dance, this weekend? *Bam!* What?!"

Diggie looks down at his hands. "Oh, wow. This is kind of awkward. Um, I just don't feel that way about you. So . . . sorry." He walks off before I can reply.

I'm kind of shocked. This is so so bad. Maddie is going to kill me.

"Michael would've *nailed* that," Joey whispers to me, appearing out of nowhere.

Parker

So my entire kid-sized head is in the fridge. What can I say? I'm thirsty!

"Hey!" says Joey, entering the kitchen.

I close the fridge door and look at him.

"There is some major twin drama going down," Joey says gleefully. "It is the perfect opportunity to complete the bro cave! Think big. Shock me!"

I think about it and say, "Maybe we should . . . take a car and drive to Vegas!"

"We are *not driving to Vegas!*" Joey says, exasperated.

"Fine!" I say, annoyed. I look slyly at the fridge. That would be a nice piece of machinery to have in the bro cave. "I do get a little thirsty eating all that popcorn," I say, tapping the fridge. "Maybe we should take this with us."

Joey smiles. "Now that little rat brain of yours is clickin'."

Rat brain? Hey, I'll take it!

Joey

Bro cave is complete! But it was a little trickier dragging a two-hundred-pound fridge up the stairs than one might think. Here's a tip: Take the milk out of the fridge before you start moving it. And the eggs.

Now Parker and I are back in the kitchen, filling ice trays at the kitchen sink to carry back upstairs. We really should start a business making bro caves.

Dad walks in. "Hey, fellas, I need to talk to you," he says.

Me and Parker exchange looks. We are so busted.

"It's been an honor, soldier," I whisper to Parker, taking his free hand.

"Are you guys holding up okay? I know your mother and I have been a little distracted with Liv and Maddie," Dad says, looking concerned. He places a hand on the wall where the fridge used to be. He doesn't notice the gaping space where the fridge usually is. We may have gotten away with taking it after all.

Me and Parker breathe sighs of relief.

"We're cool," Parker says.

"You just keep taking care of those two troublemakers," I tell Dad. "Don't give us another thought."

Dad grumbles and strolls into the living room.

"You're the best!" I call after him. Once he's gone, I sigh again.

Back to business.

"Now let go of my hand!" says Parker.

"Shhh!" I say. "Let's go."

After school, Mom calls a family meeting. Ugh.
Family meetings are the worst. Mom created family
meetings as a "forum for everyone to share their
feelings." So boring. Luckily, Dad added a shot clock.
Each person gets ten seconds to say what's on his or
her mind; then Dad blows an air horn to signal time's
up. It might sound silly, but it totally makes those
meetings more fun! Not to mention it kind of makes
me feel like I'm on the court with seconds left before
the buzzer. Sigh.

Usually I have a sense of what the family meeting
is going to be about, but this time I am totally in

the dark. When I come into the living room, Liv is already seated on a chair next to Mom. Joey, Parker, and Dad plop down on the couch as I take a seat on the chair across from Liv. She looks really nervous. That's is a first!

"Liv has something she wants to talk about," Mom announces. "So go ahead, honey. We're listening."

This is weird. I thought Liv hated family meetings as much as I did.

"Um, I was just going to have a private chat with Mom. But since we're all here, let me just say it is *snap-tastic* to be home with my fam." She snaps her fingers. "I missed you guys so much. So very, very, very, very, very, very—"

Dad blows the air horn.

We all flinch.

"Much," Liv says with a smile.

"Wait, honey, *that's* what you wanted to talk about?" Mom asks, taking Liv's hand. "It's sweet and all but a *gross* misuse of the family meeting."

Joey nods. "Yeah, I thought you were going to tell Maddie—"

Liv grabs the air horn from Dad and blows it in Joey's face.

"That you talked to Diggie—" Joey continues.

Liv blows the air horn again.

"About the dance—" Joey says.

Liv blows the air horn again and Dad snatches it from her.

"Liv," I say, "what is he talking about?"

Liv looks so guilty. She takes a deep breath and blurts out, "Maddie-I-pretended-to-be-you-and-asked-Diggie-to-the-dance-and-he-said-he-doesn't-like-you-in-that-way-ha-ha-ha! It-feels-good-to-get-it-off-my-chest-who's-next?"

"What?" I can feel my face getting hot and red. How could she do this to me? She's been back a day and she's already made everything all about her and now she's ruined my life. I just want her to go away and leave my life alone!

Parker speaks. "Hang on, Maddie, my turn. What I want to know is why I can't poop with the door *open*? Literally everyone in this house has changed my diaper. *What* are we running from, people?"

I ignore him and stare at Liv. *"You pretended to be me?"* I say.

"Maddie, I promise I was just trying to help you," Liv says.

"You were not trying to help," I say. "I told you to leave Diggie alone! But the great *Liv Rooney* had to come in and try to fix my life. Well, guess what? My life doesn't need fixing. It was so much easier being your sister when you were two thousand miles away! Ugh! I wish you never came home!"

"Maddie!" Mom says, clearly appalled at my outburst.

Liv looks like she is going to cry. "Fine!" she yells. "I'll go back!"

"Liv!" Dad says, clearly upset by Liv's reaction.

"Good! Go!" I storm into the kitchen while Liv stomps upstairs.

"So, where exactly did we land on Parker leaving the door open?" I hear Joey say as I slam the door. "I'd like to go on record as having voted 'no.'"

Joey

Me and Parker are hanging in our super cool bro cave. No big deal.

"Liv moving back to Hollywood means all eyes will be back on us," Parker tells me.

I let this little bit of sad information sink in.

I frown and say, "Which means we have to dismantle the bro cave." I feel my eyes watering. "I'm going to miss it." Better act quickly. I pick up the inflatable chair and a set of bongos and head into the hall to take them back down to the garage. It's only right. I don't want Mom and Dad getting any more upset today.

But right before I get to the stairs, Mom walks into

the hallway. I look around frantically, but I can't find a good spot to hide. So I set the chair down, sit on it, and start playing the bongos, like this is just another normal day in the life.

"Everything okay, Joey?" Mom asks me.

"Never better, baby," I say calmly between bongo flourishes.

She nods and heads down the hall to the girls' bedroom.

Liv

"Liv, honey, can we talk?" Mom says, knocking on my door. When I don't answer, she opens the door and comes in, interrupting my packing.

"Mom, you're not changing my mind!" I say, pulling clothes out of my dresser and shoving them into my sparkly suitcase. I just got my wardrobe organized and now I have to repack it all. Life is so unfair sometimes.

"Liv, are you sure that moving back to Hollywood is the best idea?" Mom asks gently, pulling my clothes out of my suitcase.

"Mom, I lived with Aunt Dena for four years. It was better for everyone," I tell her before starting on the closet. I remember how Maddie helped me unpack, and I feel kind of horrible I upset her so much. On second thought, I don't feel kind of horrible. I remind myself that I was only trying to help her with Diggie.

"I understand, but let's dialogue it out and we'll all make a decision together," Mom says, "as a family. We just got you back. I don't think your dad and I want you leaving again without you really giving this a try."

"I did give it a try!" I say. "I tried to connect with Maddie, but I just made her mad. And then, when I tried to do something nice to fix it, it just made her madder. It's like she doesn't have any room for me in her life anymore and she doesn't even want to make room."

"Oh, honey." Mom pulls me into a hug. "I know Maddie wants you here. It's just going to take a little time for both of you to adjust. This is a big change. You guys need to talk it out. Running away from this won't fix anything, I'm sure of it."

"Well, Mom, I haven't been this sure of anything since I said teal was going to be the hot color for summer." I zip up my suitcase and head for the door.

Maddie

I'm in our driveway shooting free throws, which usually makes me feel better. But it isn't working, even though I've made the last ten shots in a row. That should make me happy, but it doesn't. I wonder if Diggie is ever going to talk to me again now that Liv's ruined my chances of ever having anything special with him.

"This girl is *en fuego*!" says a voice.

I spin around and see that it's Diggie.

I jump. "Oh, uh, h-hey," I stammer.

Diggie rubs his face nervously. "Maddie, I need to talk to you. I want you to know why I said no about the dance."

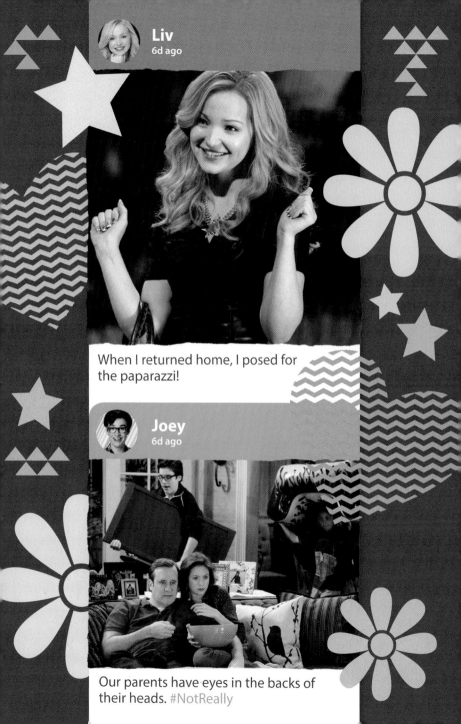

Liv
6d ago

When I returned home, I posed for the paparazzi!

Joey
6d ago

Our parents have eyes in the backs of their heads. #NotReally

Joey
5d ago

Well, Dad doesn't seem to notice the fridge is missing. So that's good.

Maddie
5d ago

At the family meeting, I kind of told Liv I wished she never came home. #Oops

Liv
5d ago

I couldn't find Maddie for the life of me, so I asked Diggie.

Maddie
5d ago

I really didn't want Liv to leave me.
I love my sis.

Parker & Joey
5d ago

I guess we should clean that up.

Liv & Maddie
5d ago

We are sisters and friends for life!

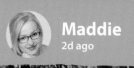

Maddie
2d ago

My basketball teammates needed to clean up their act.

Maddie
2d ago

As the new captain, I went on the defense for my team.

Liv
1d ago

Naturally, I was nominated to make Maddie's team shine!

Liv
1d ago

I helped my sister and her teammates find their inner warriors! #Dazzleberry

Maddie
1d ago

The principal shut down our team—again!
#SoNotCool

Maddie
3h ago

My team and I marched into battle—and
we looked good doing it!

Maddie
3h ago

I couldn't have rallied the team without my sis!

Liv
2h ago

My work was done. So I told Maddie I was quitting the team. *Obviously.*

"Well, this couldn't get any more awkward," I say with a nervous smile.

Joey appears, pushing Parker on a box carrier. They pass by Diggie and me. Joey says, "Out of our way! We have got a bro cave to dismantle!" before disappearing with Parker around the corner.

"Whaddya know? Got more awkward," I say jokingly.

"I said no because I knew it was Liv," Diggie says.

"What?" I ask him.

"Yeah, she didn't do that cute thing you do with your charm bracelet when you're nervous," Diggie says, looking down at my wrist. I've been spinning my charm bracelet around and around without even noticing this whole time. I drop it immediately, but I know that I am totally blushing. I laugh and snort. So not cute.

"I'm an athlete. I don't get nervous," I say, trying to sound confident instead of horribly embarrassed.

"I know you, Maddie," he says gently, reaching out and tugging on my bracelet. "Your sister has the same face, but I know you."

I smile at him calmly, but inside I am squealing and doing my happy dance.

"So, Rooney, want to go to that dance?" Diggie asks.

"Yes!" I say. Then I playfully punch his bicep. "Just so we're clear, though, I won this, right?"

He laughs. "No, I win because I get to take you to the dance."

"Aww." I grin at him. "That's what losers say!" I shove my basketball at him. "*Bam!* What?!"

He laughs. "You know, in a weird way, we have Liv to thank for this."

"Wow, you're right." I gasp. "Liv! I have to stop her." I can't believe I said such mean things to her. She really has been trying to help. There is no way I can let her leave. I run toward the house but stop before I get to the door. I turn back to Diggie and yell, "Oh, by the way, I'm not wearing a dress to that dance."

Diggie smiles and shoots me a thumbs-up. Then he yells in his sports announcer voice, *"And there she goes, folks. She's going . . . going . . . gone!"*

I'm obviously not going to stay where I'm not wanted, and if Maddie doesn't want me here, then this just isn't home anymore.

I drag one of my suitcases downstairs, with Mom right behind me. I don't really have a plan for how to get back to Hollywood, but I can make that up on the fly, right? I'm an actress, after all. Improv is second nature to me.

Dad stops me in the living room. "Liv, if you're leaving, you should probably take this with you." He hands me a pink sparkly picture frame. Inside is the art project Maddie and I made in second grade. I haven't seen it in years. It's a drawing of the two of us together, and above it, we wrote: *Sisters by chance, friends by choice.*

Mom puts her arm around me and looks over my shoulder. "Wow, remember when you two made that? 'Sisters by chance, friends by choice.'"

"So corny . . ." I let out a little laugh, but I can't help reaching out and touching Maddie's handwriting. I just want us to be friends again.

"Liv, twins are special," Dad says. "Since the day you were born, it's never *just* been Liv, and it's never *just* been Maddie. It's always been *Liv and Maddie.*"

"She'll always be your sister," Mom adds, "but it's tough to be best friends when you're two thousand miles away."

It's all too much. I start crying. "What, you think I'm going to just fall to pieces over a second-grade art project?" I sniffle.

Maddie. What have I done? I clutch the frame and head out to find her. When I reach the backyard, Diggie is there playing basketball. But my sister is nowhere to be found.

"Where's Maddie?" I ask. Diggie says she's inside, so I turn and run right back into the house

I race into the kitchen and through it to the living room. I have to find Liv and stop her from leaving. What if I'm too late? What if I can never get her to move back home?

"Where's Liv?" I ask when I find Mom and Dad standing in the living room.

"She just left," Mom says. I race toward the front door, but Mom stops me. "No, she went out back to find you."

I glare at her. "You could have been a little clearer when I asked the first time!" I turn and head toward the back.

I push through the kitchen door and run smack into Liv. Ouch! We both stagger backward, rubbing our heads.

"Liv!"

"Maddie!"

"I have to talk to you!" I say.

"I have to talk to *you*!" she says, panting. "You first. I have to catch my breath. I don't usually do my own stunts."

"Liv, I'm so sorry," I say, shaking my head. "What I said was mean. I'm totally psyched you came back from Hollywood. I'm sorry."

"No, you were right," Liv says. "I shouldn't have tried to fix your life. I'm sorry."

"Don't be sorry! Diggie asked me to the dance!" I exclaim.

Liv squeals and I join in. "Get this: he only said no to me because he knew it was you."

Liv scoffs. "*Knew it was me?* No way. I do you better than you do you. *Bam!* Who?!" She pauses. "Wait, is it '*Bam!* What?!'?"

I laugh. This is exactly what I was excited about

when I found out she was moving home—I finally have my best friend back.

Liv hands me the frame she's been holding. I can't believe it—it's our second-grade art project.

I gasp. "No way! I remember when we made this. 'Sisters by chance. Friends by choice.' So corny." I reach out, take her hand, and give it a squeeze.

"So corny," Liv says, and squeezes my hand back.

"Liv, please don't leave," I beg, trying not to cry.

"You couldn't drag me away," Liv says. I can see tears in her eyes, too.

I pull her into a hug. Over her shoulder I can see Mom and Dad watching us in the doorway.

"Oh, I'm going to . . ." Mom whispers, her eyes shimmering.

"Hold it together," Dad says as tears roll down his cheeks. "We don't want to spoil this perfect moment."

I start to tell them to quit being so embarrassing, but just then the fridge crashes down the back stairs, followed by our popcorn machine. Popcorn and sodas fly everywhere. Liv and I shriek and duck under the table, and Dad blocks Mom from the worst of it.

When the popcorn settles, we see Joey and Parker standing wide-eyed at the top of the stairs.

"To Vegas!" Parker yells.

"Right there with you, buddy," Joey says, nodding. Then they both turn and run.

Ugh. My brothers truly are the worst. And kind of hysterical.

"**Parker!** If you're not going to close the door, at least don't make eye contact!" I yell as I walk into the living room, having passed the hall bath. Parker is in there, on the toilet with the door open. Again. Little brothers are seriously so gross.

"It's only weird if you make it weird!" Parker yells back.

I roll my eyes at Mom and Dad, who are on the couch watching TV.

The doorbell rings and I rush to answer it. It's Diggie, all dressed up in a suit and tie and ready to take Maddie to the dance. Yay! I am so excited for her!

"Your starting lineup for tonight's dance: Diggie and Maddie!" Diggie announces in his booming voice.

"Yeah, that's cute," Dad says sternly, trying to look intimidating. "Have her home by eleven."

"Okay," Diggie says quickly. I guess Dad can be pretty scary.

"Maddie, Diggie's here!" I call up the stairs. "Just wait until you see her!" I tell him. I've been helping Maddie get ready for hours, and she looks gorgeous. Diggie won't know what hit him!

Maddie slowly starts down the stairs. She is wearing a light blue dress with a full tulle skirt and high heels, although she is a little wobbly with each step. Her hair and makeup are absolutely flawless. Even her glasses look extra fancy.

"Whoa. I think I swallowed my gum," Diggie says, looking stunned.

"You look like an angel, honey," Mom says, snapping pictures.

"You're gorgeous, Mads," Dad says proudly.

"Am I a miracle worker?" I ask. "A little bit."

"It's picture time. Come on down," Mom says.

Maddie sighs and grimaces. "I can't. I'm sorry, Diggie, I just can't." She turns and wobbles back up the stairs.

"What a diva," I say, laughing.

Dad takes Diggie by the elbow and steers him toward the door. "You heard the girl. She changed her mind. Beat it."

But before Diggie can leave, Maddie bounds back down the stairs wearing her dress with basketball shoes. "Much better," she says happily.

Diggie smiles at her.

"Maddie, it's a dance," I protest. "You can't wear—"

"Hey," Maddie says, cutting me off. "I put on a dress. Don't push it."

I laugh. I've learned my lesson. I'm not going to push it.

I'm just glad to have my sister back exactly as she is.

PART
TWO ♥

"Good morning, fellow Rooneys!" I sing out,
walking ever so dramatically down the kitchen stairs
for breakfast. Maddie, Joey, and Mom are eating
cereal at the kitchen table. Dad and Parker are
packing a lunch. "Today is the first day of the rest
of your lives . . . with me!" I say, clasping my hands
together and grinning.

Maddie laughs and rolls her eyes.

"Hey, Hollywood," Joey says. "Tomorrow, less time
in the shower. You used up all the hot water. Makes it
really hard to shave."

Maddie and I give him skeptical looks.

Joey says, "That's right, guys. I shave." He stretches

and puts his hands behind his head, trying to look cool. "Spread the word."

Parker shrugs. "Didn't bother me. I took a shower with the hose out front."

"Weren't you worried about someone seeing you?" I ask, appalled.

"Oh, come on, like the neighbors haven't seen that already!" Parker says. He and Dad join Maddie, Joey, and Mom at the kitchen table.

I take a bowl of cereal from the counter and look for a seat at the kitchen table, but all the chairs are taken and I do *not* eat standing up like a farm animal. "Um, what happened to my chair?" I ask with my signature sweet smile.

"Ooh," says Maddie. "Um, Parker broke it over Joey's back when they were wrestling."

"Correction," Joey says. "*He* was wrestling. *I* was eating soup."

Mom glares at Parker. "You know, this is ridiculous. You shouldn't have to stand to eat your breakfast. Joey, get her a seat."

Joey hops up and slides the kitchen trash can to the

table. He taps it and looks up at me. "Welcome home, Hollywood."

I sit down ever so sadly.

"You know," I say with my nose scrunched up, "when I asked you guys to treat me like a regular person, I didn't *really* mean it."

Maddie

I cross the finish line and Dad clicks his
stopwatch to mark my time. We finish every
basketball practice with a timed mile. I'm the first
one back, as usual.

"A twelve-minute mile, Maddie?" Dad says with
disapproval. "What happened?"

"I ran two!" I say, feeling my pulse.

Dad stares at me, impressed.

The rest of the team jogs in.

My teammate Cassie runs over to me.

"Nice, Cassie! Personal best," Dad tells her.

Cassie pants and nods. "Last time I walked, because

I didn't want to get a blister," she says. "But I ran this time, 'cause I was chased by a squirrel."

Stains appears. She is soaked and her gym clothes are smeared with dirt.

"Look at you, Stains," Dad says. "Working up a sweat."

"A school bus ran through a puddle and splashed me," Stains says, pulling at her wet tank top. Not that it's a big deal, but Stains is always dirty somehow.

Dad blows his whistle and gestures to the rest of the team in the distance. "Team meeting, everybody! Grab some water. Hustle it up, Willow! Hustle up!"

Willow and the rest of the girls stagger over the finish line and join us. Willow immediately kicks off her sneakers, pulls the lid off the watercooler, and dunks her feet directly into the cold water. "Ahh, heaven," Willow moans with a smile. "My dogs have been barking since Sycamore Street." She looks up at the rest of the team, who look very thirsty and a little bit annoyed. "Oh, wait, were you guys using this?" Willow is the strongest girl on our team, and she is always complaining about her sore feet—always.

"Okay," Dad says to us. "Don't forget, team retreat at my house this weekend. Also, your votes are in and the Ridgewood High Fighting Porcupines have themselves a new team captain!"

We all cheer and clap.

"She's the first sophomore ever chosen," Dad says. "Maddie Rooney!"

The girls all mob me to give me hugs, patting my back.

I can't believe it! Well, yes I can. Basketball is my life. And being named captain of the team is *huge* for me. And I may be playing it cool in front of the girls on the team, but I also may go home later and squeal in my closet. Eee!

"Way to go, Maddie," Willow says, walking toward me. "Chest bump."

I step back. "Not the . . ."

Willow rushes at me, bumping her chest into mine and knocking me to the ground.

". . . chest bump," I gasp. Willow is a *lot* stronger than me. Her chest bumps are epic—and not in the good way. Ouch.

"You're going to be a great captain, Maddie," Cassie says cheerfully, helping me up, "unless you're really bad and the whole team turns against you."

I guess I haven't thought of that. Let's hope that doesn't happen! After all, I'm proud to be captain of such a great team, despite that Liv thinks the girls on the team are all kind of like the "before" in a makeover show, which she says means they have potential. I think that's just Liv's way of giving a compliment.

We all head toward the locker room (we make Willow carry the foot water) and pass the statue of our school mascot, Paulie the Fighting Porcupine. Principal Fickman is in the middle of pulling a party hat and a feather boa off the statue.

"Uh, Principal Fickman, what are you doing?" I ask him. "Is it Paulie the Porcupine's birthday?"

Principal Fickman snorts. "It most certainly is not. Someone out there thinks it's a big hee-haw to keep dressing up the mascot while I'm neither hee-ing nor haw-ing!"

"You gotta admit, it is kind of funny." Dad laughs

until he sees that Principal Fickman is glaring at him; then he adopts a stern expression. "It's a travesty, sir."

"We've had to make some budget cuts, and girls' basketball got hit hard," says the principal. "The good news is I got you the new uniforms you requested." The principal picks up a bag that was leaning against the base of the statue, and dumps grayish uniforms out of it onto the hall floor.

We all squeal happily and then reach down and pick up uniform pieces.

"The bad news is," says the principal, "they're the boys' old uniforms, sweaty and unlaundered."

We immediately drop the uniforms. So gross.

"No, we need new uniforms!" I protest. "We're going to a tournament in Chicago."

"Yeah," says Dad. "The Walter Worciechowski Invitational! It took me three days to learn how to say it."

Principal Fickman shrugs with a nasty sneer on his face. "What can I say? Money's tight. I'm only funding things the student body cares about."

"People care about girls' basketball!" I tell him.

He bursts into an evil little laugh. "Sure they do," he says meanly. "You keep telling yourself that."

"Principal Fickman, we're not going to let you treat us this way. Right, team?" I say confidently, waiting for my team to back me up. He'll have to listen if we all speak up loudly enough. But no one makes a sound. I turn around and see all the girls looking uncomfortably to the sides and down at their shoes. I sigh.

"Wow, it's as quiet in here as the gym during a girls' basketball game," Principal Fickman says. "Well, if you'll excuse me, I promised Mother I'd be home in time for *Wheel of Fortune*."

I smile sweetly. There is more than one way to win a fight. "Principal Fickman, before you go, would you like a nice, cold glass of water?" I fill up a cup with the dirty foot water from the cooler and hand it to him.

He gulps it down. "Refreshing!" he says.

Once the principal walks off and is out of sight, I turn to Willow and say, "Please tell me you still have athlete's foot."

"Raging," she assures me.

"Good girl," I say, and give her a high five.

But even though we won the battle, we haven't won the war.

And I'm kind of upset that my team didn't back me up.

What's that about?

I think about Cassie's words, about the team turning on me.

We'd better find our team spirit—and fast.

But how?

Joey

I'm seated at the kitchen table after school working on algebra when Parker sneaks up behind me.

"Hey, Joey!" Parker says.

He holds up a plastic cage with a large, furry tarantula inside it.

I let out a scream. "What are you doing with a tarantula?" I ask him.

Parker laughs. "Her name is Sylvia, and she's the class pet. I'm taking care of them for the weekend."

"Them? Parker, I only see the one," I say.

"Yeah . . ." Parker says. "I already lost the other five when I let them out of the cage."

"*What?* Why would you let them out of their cage?" I say.

I look around frantically. My skin prickles as if there were spiders on me.

"Duh," Parker says matter-of-factly. "To train them for the *all-tarantula circus*!"

I give Parker a stern look. "Parker, you are so irresponsible!" Then I stick my lower lip out in a pout. "How could you not invite me to your tarantula circus?"

Just then a tarantula appears on the kitchen table.

I scream again.

Parker calmly places a cereal bowl over it, delighted. "Caught one! It's either Julie, the trapeze artist, or Bernardo, the sword swallower. Four more to go."

I shudder. Then I hear a horn honk from the driveway. I look out the window and say, "Parker, that's Mom! You cannot tell her anything about this, okay? If she finds out that there's a bunch of spiders crawling around, she will *freak* out. Okay, here she comes. Act natural." I place my hand under my chin.

Parker hides his tarantula cage on a chair and leans on me.

Okay. Not so natural.

Mom walks in through the door with groceries.

I hope she doesn't lift the cereal bowl off the kitchen table.

"Oh, hi, boys," Mom says sweetly. "Listen, Maddie's basketball team is going to be here all weekend." She places her grocery bags on the island.

The cereal bowl moves across the kitchen table. Parker and I stare at it.

"Hey, hey, hey! Eyes on me," says Mom, not seeming to notice it. "So this weekend, don't cause any trouble, okay?"

"Trouble?" Parker scoffs. "Who do you think you're talking to, lady?" When Mom glares at him, he gives a flourish of his hand and says, "Milady."

After school, Maddie and I head up to our bedroom to do our homework.

Homework, oh, how I haven't missed you. Sigh.

I put it away, hop onto my bed, and start applying this killer new mascara that makes my eyes seem twice as big. I have this super-cute pink glittery compact mirror that makes applying makeup on the fly totally easy.

Maddie starts exercising with resistance bands and venting to me about basketball. Basketball. It's such a cute sport, with adorable matching tanks and shorts. It's a shame Maddie's team doesn't have any cutesy uniforms. The principal really pulled a number on her and her team. I feel bad for her, mostly because she dribbles a ball for hours at a time and thinks it's actually fun.

Maddie is so flustered she's having trouble stringing words together.

"No one on the team had my back," she says. "It's so . . ."

"Frust-a-pointing," I finish for her, pressing on more mascara.

Maddie pauses. "That's not a real word, yet somehow I know exactly what it means." She goes back to using her resistance bands. "How do you do that?"

I smile. "It's a gift."

Maddie sighs. "Maybe I'm just not cut out to be captain. I have no idea what to do."

"I do," I say confidently, shutting my compact mirror.

Maddie snort-laughs. "Please! You don't have a *clue* about basketball." She folds up her resistance bands.

I smile and say, "Maddie, this is about leadership. On *Sing It Loud!*"—I sing it, per usual—"my cast was a team and I led them through four critically acclaimed seasons of television." I feel pride swelling within me. I sit up straight on the bed and grin at Maddie, who's now on her bed. "Want to know how I did it?"

"No," Maddie says sarcastically.

I ignore her. "Okay, there are five steps of leadership. One: grab their attention. Two: get them on the same page. Three: identify your goal. Four: lead them into battle. And five: look great doing it." I smile and let out a dreamy sigh.

Maddie thinks for a moment, then says, "Okay, if I imagine those words *not* coming out of *your* mouth, they actually kind of make sense."

I clap, smile, and try not to be offended by that last part, especially since she's had such a rough day. I continue. "Okay, step one: grab their attention." I stand and give jazz hands. "In Hollywood, they always say the best way to do that is by firing someone on your first day of work."

"Liv, I'm not firing any of my friends," Maddie says adamantly.

I roll my eyes. "Ugh. Do I have to connect all the dots for you? I will join the team and you can fire *me* for being terrible. The team will know you mean business if you're ruthless enough to crush your twin's fake dream!"

"Liv, that's actually kind of brilliant," Maddie says, standing up. Then her face breaks into a huge grin. "And I do love the idea of firing you!"

This morning, the entire girls' basketball team—*my* team—convenes at my house for our weekend retreat. We're standing in the driveway in the backyard with Dad. I'm really excited to implement Liv's plan and get the team behind me.

Dad is definitely in full-on coaching mode. He blows his whistle and booms, "Listen up, Lady Porcupines, we have the tournament in Chicago in three weeks. This retreat is about coming together and becoming a real team."

I step forward and say, "Yeah, that means if a girl puts herself out on the line, like, say, in front of the principal, you better back her up! So to get us started, I got us all team bracelets!" I hold up blue rubber bracelets with "Got Your Back" printed on them. I hand one to each of my teammates and slip one onto my own wrist.

"'Got Your Back,'" Cassie reads. She smiles.

"Cool," Stains says, fiddling with her bracelet. It snaps. "Mine broke."

"You know what, it's okay," I tell her. "I have plenty extra. I had to buy, like, five hundred to get the discount."

Dad clears his throat.

"I mean, *my dad* had to buy five hundred," I say, correcting myself.

"Thank you," Dad says. "Now how 'bout some passing drills?"

"Hold up, Dad," I say. "One more thing. We have a new teammate."

"Great!" Dad says. "Can she play center? We got no D if Willow goes down."

"Willow doesn't *go* down!" Willow shouts, giving me a high five.

I press on. "Please, everybody, welcome, all the way from Hollywood . . . Livvvvv Rooney!"

Liv walks out of the house, waving at us. She's dressed in a skirt, a red blouse, and three-inch-high heels. She clasps her hands together and bows. "Thank you! It is an *honor* to be nominated in the same category as these *other* very talented women." She gives us all her made-for-TV twinkly-eyed smile.

The whole team breaks into a light smattering of applause, although they look like they aren't sure why they're clapping.

"Well, okayyyy," Dad says, sounding confused. "Welcome aboard, Liv!" He throws the basketball he's been holding to Liv, who shrieks and jumps out of the ball's path instead of catching it.

I bite my lip and hang my head. Maybe this wasn't such a great idea.

"Well, at least we'll have someone who can sing the national anthem," Dad says cheerfully.

"So, Hollywood big shot, what position do you play?" Willow asks her.

Liv laughs like the answer is obvious. "I'm usually the lead," she says.

After an hour of not-so-amazing practice in the driveway, I feel like Maddie and I have kept up this adorable little charade for long enough. I've been lying in a lounge chair watching the girls doing drills. It's such a snooze. But at least I'm helping out Maddie. Dad blows his whistle as they finish another drill and all high-five each other.

"Great job, team!" Dad says. "Anybody need water?"

Everyone looks at the watercooler. It's the same cooler Willow stuck her stinky feet in yesterday—yeah, Maddie told me all about it during her venting session earlier—so there is no way anyone here is going to drink that nasty water.

"Dad, we seriously need a new watercooler," Maddie tells him.

"Not in the budget," Dad says. Then he grimaces, looking at the foot cooler. "We've got some juice boxes in the garage. I'll go find them. Captain's in charge."

As Dad heads off, Maddie takes control. "Okay, everybody, let's start with some layups. Liv, you first. Catch." She's about to throw the basketball to me.

I hold up a hand, wrinkle my nose, and shake my head dramatically. "No, sorry. I'm not touching that ball. It's heavy and it's just such a boring color."

"Liv, being on this team requires hard work! And if you're not up for that, then maybe you're not cut out for this," Maddie says confidently, just like we practiced. Everyone on the team holds her breath.

"Wait. Are you"—I stand and face her and the girls—"kicking me off the team?"

All the girls look at each other like they're shocked this is happening.

Now I really lay it on thick. "I'm devastated," I say. "Devastated!"

"Liv, *I'm* the captain. I've made my decision. Now go," Maddie says firmly, pointing to the house.

The whole team gasps. They've been watching our back-and-forth intently. I don't think they thought she'd really cut me from the team. Attention officially grabbed! Step one complete. I am so proud of her! Her acting is excellent—almost as good as mine! Almost.

"I see," I say, sniffling like I am going to cry. "Don't cry for me, Lady Porcupines. I'll be all right. . . ." I sigh and walk toward the house. "Somehow."

"You can't kick Liv off the team!" Willow tells Maddie.

I stop walking. That wasn't supposed to happen.

"*I can't?*" Maddie asks.

"*She can't?*" I echo.

Cassie nods. "Willow's right. Liv is *terrible*, but she'll learn. We all had to."

"Yeah, she's our teammate now," Stains says. "We have to back her up. Just like you said, man," she says to Maddie, pointing to the "Got Your Back" bracelets.

"I did say that, didn't I?" Maddie says slowly. She

gives me a look and shrugs. "Uh, okay. Liv, I guess you are . . . back on the team."

"Yay!" I say weakly, raising an arm halfheartedly. It is time to think of a plan B, because there is no way I am actually going to play basketball all season.

Or at all, let's be honest.

Maddie

Tonight the whole team has crashed in sleeping bags on our living room floor. It has been really cool having this retreat, but I can't sleep. I'm too worried about how Liv and I are going to get her off the team. Liv promised she had an idea, but we haven't had a chance to talk alone, so here I am, tossing and turning.

A light catches my eye. I see Parker and Joey wearing headlamps and holding butterfly nets. They are crawling across the floor and looking for something. *"The itsy-bitsy spider went up the water spout,"* they sing softly.

I sit up. Whatever they are doing seems pretty funny, but I can't let them pull any pranks with my team if that's what this is about. "Crashing a girls' sleepover? Not cool, brahs," I whisper to them.

Joey laughs nervously. "Ah, you caught us. We were trying to cause mischief."

I can tell he's lying, but he can't do anything now that he knows I'm awake, so I'll let it go. "Great. Now I'm awake. I need a snack," I say, and stand up.

"Is it cool if we look through your sleeping bag while you're gone?" Parker asks me.

"I don't know what you're looking for, but I do know you look stupid doing it," I say. I shake my head, walk into the kitchen, and find Liv making tea.

"Liv, what are you doing in *here*?" I ask.

"Oh, I don't sleep in bags," Liv says.

Typical Liv.

"So listen," she says, "I'm sorry my plan kind of backfired and blew up in our faces today."

I shake my head. "Liv, what are you talking about? I mean, I know it didn't go the way we thought it would, but . . . when I saw the team rally around you, I saw *passion* for the first time."

Liv looks relieved. She sets down her mug of tea and claps. "Faboosh! We are now officially ready for step two."

"Remind me what step two is again," I say.

"Getting the team on the same page," Liv says.

"Perfect," I say. "First thing in the morning, we—"

A scream from the living room cuts me off. "TARANTULA!"

All the girls thunder into the kitchen, screaming and brushing off their pajamas, then race into the backyard. Parker and Joey enter the kitchen. Parker has a tarantula caught in his butterfly net. "Yes! Caught another one: Joan, the troubled ringmaster from a broken home," he says, admiring his catch.

"A broken home?" Joey asks. "Was it divorce?"

Parker shakes his head. "No, I literally stepped on her home."

Ugh, brother. I'll have to make this up to my team.

I'll compliment them on their hustle. That'll do the trick.

This morning, Maddie and I are going to put our plan into action. I wait until the girls are out on the court and ready to warm up, and I watch and listen for my cue.

"Okay, guys," Maddie says. Then she sees them stretching and nearly falling over doing so. "Guys! Come on! You call these warm-ups?" she says. "The first thing any opposing team is going to see from *us* is how we warm up, right? They need to know that we think as one, play as one, and win as one."

Think as one, play as one, win as one—that's my cue!

"We'll still go to the bathroom on our own, though, right?" Cassie asks.

I walk out onto the deck dressed in a leotard and

tights and carrying a heavy carved walking stick. I thump my stick on the deck a few times to get the team's attention. "I want you all to reach deep into your soul and find your *inner warrior*," I call loudly. "Who is she?" I point my cane at Cassie. "What makes her so fierce?" I point it at Willow, then at Maddie, then at the rest of the team. "What accessories can we use to highlight . . . that fierceness?"

The girls begin to nod.

"I have no clue what she's saying, but I'm listening because she seems confident and she carries a big stick," Stains tells Willow.

I walk theatrically down the steps of the deck so that I'm standing right in front of the girls. I press my cane onto the pavement. "Take a moment," I say.

The girls stare at me, clearly confused. Okay, they're not getting it.

"Close your eyes!" I tell them. They do. Maddie sneaks over to me.

"*I thought we were just doing new warm-ups . . .*" Maddie whispers to me, sounding puzzled.

"It's a process!" I say, smiling. She should trust me. I'm a pro!

Joey

Mom opens the kitchen cabinet and screams when she finds the dishes inside it are covered in spiderwebs. "Why are these plates all covered with cobwebs?" she asks me and Parker as we walk into the kitchen. Uh-oh. Talk about a sticky situation!

I exchange panicked looks with Parker. "Ha! That's, uh, so *weird*!" I say.

I hope I don't sound too guilty.

"Yeah, you wouldn't expect tarantulas here in Wisconsin," Parker adds.

I pull Parker close and cover his mouth. "Ix-nay on the arantula-tay."

Mom spins around and I quickly turn my choke

hold into a friendly hug. Mom doesn't notice a thing. She is too busy trying to get lunch ready for the basketball team. "I'm glad you guys are here. You can help me serve lunch," she says, pulling a huge cloth off a six-foot-long turkey hoagie on the kitchen table.

"It's beautiful!" I say, admiring the hoagie.

"I'm feeding athletes," Mom says. "I went big. Here, help me take it outside. Parker, honey, could you open the door?"

Parker opens the back door and calls, "Come and get it!"

I help Mom pick up the hoagie on a sandwich board and we carry it outside.

"Now this is for the team, but don't worry, you boys get leftovers," Mom says. Before we make it outside, the girls grab the sandwich board.

"Ladies! Don't grab at it!" Mom yells. But it's too late. It's all we can do to hold on to the sandwich board as the girls devour the hoagie like wild animals.

"At least let us set it down!" I shout.

A minute later the entire sandwich is gone. Mom

sets the board back down on the table and shakes her head. "I'm so sorry you boys had to see that."

I'm just sad I wasn't able to try a bite of that beautiful bread.

Maddie and the team huddle around in the backyard. From the deck, I'm watching them. I've been teaching them to unleash their inner warriors all afternoon. Eventually, Dad wanders out to the court wearing his bathrobe. So humiliating.

"Oh . . . this was a *two*-day retreat?" Dad says, looking very surprised.

"Yeah," Maddie says, grinning. "And we've been working on a new warm-up that we want to show you."

New warm-up—right, that's my cue!

I clap and call out to the team, "Places!"

The girls all make a straight line on the court.

"Now, remember," I say, "find your *inner warrior*. Five, six, seven, eight!"

While I stand behind the team, they perform a very intimidating martial arts–esque routine. I practice along with them. They look absolutely amazing: they are all totally in sync. They finally look and sound like a real team.

"*Bam!* What?!" Maddie yells as they finish.

Dad looks impressed. "Wow, that was ah-mazing."

Maddie high-fives the teammates. We all cheer.

"If Fickman could see you now, he'd never say no," says Dad.

I couldn't agree more.

Dad's right. We aren't going to let Principal
Fickman say no. We're getting those new uniforms.
So me and the team all head down to the school and
find Principal Fickman outside it. He's grilling steaks,
wearing an apron and a chef's hat.

I walk right up to him. "Principal Fickman, it's not
fair for you to give the boys' team new uniforms and
not the girls' team. I am here to ask—no, to *demand*—
that you give us new uniforms as well." It's a pretty
good speech if I do say so myself.

"No," he says flatly. He turns back to his grill and
flips his steaks. "Now, if you'll excuse me, I have to

finish barbecuing these exquisite steaks for the boys'
team. They are having their retreat inside."

"Unacceptable," I say firmly. "We can't go to the
Worciechowski tournament with those uniforms you
gave us."

Principal Fickman laughs meanly. "Oh, that *is* a
problem. But *I* think *I* have a solution. You're not
going to the tournament."

"*W-what?*" I stammer. "You can't do that."

He raises an eyebrow. "I think I just did." He pulls
the steaks off the grill and takes them inside just as
Dad runs up.

"You couldn't wait for me to get dressed?" Dad says,
out of breath. "Come on! Let's go get those uniforms!"

I just sigh and lead the girls back home. No
uniforms. No tournament. I'm a total failure as a
captain. I have to do something to fix it. I just don't
know what.

We all sit around in Liv's and my room a few hours
later.

Everyone is pretty gloomy, huddled on Liv's bed.

Luckily, Liv and I have found a brilliant-beyond-brilliant solution.

"Okay, guys," I say. "We were shut down by Fickman again. I know that was a real kick to the stomach. But if he's not going to help us, we're not going to sit around and cry about it, am I right? We're going to help ourselves." Then I gesture to the door of our bathroom. "Stains, would you come out here, please?"

Stains slides the door open and walks in wearing one of the boys' old blue uniforms. She doesn't look happy. She has to hold the shorts to keep them from falling down, and the shirt comes almost to her knees.

"This is what Principal Fickman thinks we're worth. Are we going to stand for this?" I say in a booming voice. "Stains, catch!" I toss a ball to Stains. As soon as she lets go of the shorts to catch the ball, they fall around her ankles.

"This. Is madness!" Stain exclaims, pointing to her fallen shorts.

Willow shakes her head. "I bet the boys don't worry about *their* pants falling off!"

"Are we going to take this sitting down?" I yell.

"Willow doesn't *go* down!" Willow shouts, making a fist.

Liv appears in the doorway, tapping her cane on the ground hard. The whole team turns to look at her.

"Attention, Lady Groundhogs!" she says dramatically.

"Um, we're the Porcupines," Cassie says, looking indignant.

"Whatever," Liv says. "Cue music!" She pulls the remote off a nearby shelf, and music starts to play. She then rips a purple silk sheet off an easel to reveal the colorful poster she made earlier.

"Behold your future uniforms," she says, pointing her cane at the poster. "The sporty sport short looks great on the court or just sitting on the bench."

"That's me!" Stains exclaims. "I sit the bench. I'm going to look great!"

Liv ignores her and clears her throat. "The b-ball tank is perfect for all that dribble-y, drabble-y, shoot-y stuff you girls like to do. Dunk-tastic, am I right?"

Willow looks at the poster longingly. "I want to get married in that."

"We need those uniforms!" Cassie says. "We can't let Fickman ruin Willow's wedding!" The girls turn to each other with nervous expressions.

Aaaand we have our common goal. Step three, achieved!

I have to admit, it's cool to see the girls so excited for once, even if it is about fashion.

"We're all ears, Captain. How do we get 'em?" Stains asks me.

I lift a bag filled with the 490 extra "Got Your Back" bracelets I've had made for the team. "This is how," I say. "We're going to raise money for *those* uniforms by selling *these* bracelets to the kids at school who *do* support us. Are you with me?"

"Yeah!" the girls yell, pumping their fists in the air.

"Are we going to tell Principal Fickman he can't push us around?!" I yell.

"Yeah!" they say, and all pump their fists again.

When Stains throws her fist up, her shorts fall down again.

"Does everyone want Stains to pull up her pants?" I yell.

"Yeah!" the girls, even Stains, call out.

Joey

I walk into the living room and find Parker on the couch. He's lowering a live cricket into his mouth. This is too weird, even for Parker.

"Parker, what are you doing? Stop!" I yell, bolting over to him.

"Eating a cricket. To catch a tarantula, you have to eat like a tarantula," Parker says. "Duh."

I take a seat beside him. "And . . . where did you hear that?" I ask.

"Oh! The man in my head," Parker says. "He comes up with all kinds of cool things."

I smile. "Oh! Okay! Yeah!" I say. "Please, carry on."

Parker lowers the cricket toward his mouth again just as Mom walks in.

"Put. The. Bug. Down!" Mom says. "What's going on?"

Parker immediately puts the cricket into a paper bucket. He looks at Mom sheepishly.

"Okay, fine," Parker says. "I'm tired of the lies. I brought home tarantulas from school, and they kinda . . . sorta . . . got out."

"*What?*" Mom asks, looking terrified.

"We caught two, but one of them got away," Parker explains.

I gasp. "Joan, the troubled ringmaster?"

Parker nods sadly. "She just can't be tied down."

Mom looks back and forth between Parker and me. She looks like she wants to scream in horror. "There are gross, hairy *tarantulas* crawling around our house somewhere? Find them. Now." She shudders and pulls at her clothes. "I know this is completely in my head, but I feel like I can feel them crawling all over me."

Mom starts to head upstairs.

She has five tarantulas clinging to her back!

I guess Parker sees them, too. He yells, "Mom!"

I immediately clamp my hand over Parker's mouth.

"What is it?" Mom turns on the step and looks at us.

"Just . . . we love you," I say, pretending to hug Parker.

"Aw, I love you guys, too," Mom says, blowing us a kiss. Then she goes on upstairs.

I put my finger up to my lips, shushing Parker. "It's better this way."

The next day I strut right up to Principal Fickman in the hallway, where he is taking a polka-dot bikini top (not a cute one) off the Paulie the Porcupine statue.

"Joke's on you, students," he mutters to himself. "Mother is going to love this!"

"Principal Fickman!" I say rather saucily.

"Too late, I've got dibs," he says, clutching the bikini top territorially.

"Okay . . ." Who'd want that tired old thing anyway? I say, "The girls' basketball team decided we weren't going to wait for you to come through for us, so we took matters into our own hands."

"Ooh, did you bake a pie?" Principal Fickman laughs.

"Are you with me, Ridgewood High?" I call over my shoulder.

Every kid in the hallway raises a hand. They are all wearing teal "Got Your Back" bracelets.

"Okay, what's going on?" Principal Fickman asks me.

"You're about to see steps four and five: marching into battle and looking good doing it. Joey, cue my jam!" I call out, raising an eyebrow at him.

Joey raises his phone above his head and presses play.

That's when the doors to the gym fly open.

Here goes nothing!

Maddie

Once the gym doors are open, I march toward the principal. Me and my team are all wearing the bejeweled new uniforms Liv designed for us. They consist of purple, teal, and silver jersey tops and shorts with our names and numbers outlined in rhinestones. We look good! *Bam!* What?!

I am also carrying a mesh sack over my shoulder. My team walks behind me. Talk about getting my back. Smoke flies around us, disco lights flash, and we march in time to Joey's music. I feel super powerful. It's a perfect moment to shine. (Well, minus Stains walking into a locker. Good thing she walked it off.) We stop right in front of Principal Fickman.

I say, "Thanks for the loaners, but we don't need these anymore." I dump the bag out at his feet. It is filled with the boys' ugly old uniforms. "*Bam!* What?!" I say sassily, exuding my Liv-esque attitude.

"You said money only goes to the things the student body cares about," Willow says. "Well, look around."

The principal gives her a blank stare.

"I said *look*!" Willow bellows. That's my girl.

The principal's eyes widen.

"She meant look *please*," Stains says. "We're working on manners."

Principal Fickman grimaces like he smells something bad. Probably the boys' uniforms. "I hate to say it, but I have a new respect for you girls. Ha-ha. Really hate to say it," he says through gritted teeth, looking crestfallen.

"Are you going to send us to the Worciechowski tournament?" I ask him.

I hold my breath. I feel my whole team holding their breath.

Principal Fickman sighs. "I could find room in budget for that."

Everyone in the hallway cheers. I flash Liv a smile.

"All right, make way, people," says the principal. "I have to get to the yearbook folks and tell them I'm just going to print last year's edition again. Sorry ninth graders, you lose." Principal Fickman walks away down the hall.

Joey laughs. Then his expression hardens. "Wait . . . I'm a ninth grader," he says. "That was the best picture I've ever taken!" He hurries down the hall after Principal Fickman. "Wait! Please stop! No!"

"Nice work!" Willow tells me. "My porcupine quills feel a little sharper because of you, Captain!" She gives me two super-hard high fives.

"We really have to thank Liv." I smile as I walk over to my sis, no doubt looking as proud as I feel. "I can't believe I'm saying this, but you are the best teammate I've ever had," I tell Liv. "I mean, I never could have rallied the team without you."

"Oh, Maddie, that's so sweet," Liv says kindly. Then she says in a more serious tone and lowly so only I can hear her, "We both know I'm quitting, right?"

"I already cleaned out your fake locker," I assure her.

Dad runs in. "Maddie! I have a great idea! We should sell those extra bracelets you ordered and use the money to buy new uniforms," he says.

I point at my new uniform.

"Oh, come on! I'm the coach. You gotta keep me in the loop!" Dad says.

I turn to my team. "All right, Fighting Porcupines. Let's bounce." I wrap my arm around Liv's shoulders and we walk, side by side, down the hall with the team.

We may have gotten off to a rough start, Liv and I, but we are already back to being an unstoppable team.

It is going to be such a great year.

Bam! What?!

TEAM LIV AND MADDIE

SISTERS FOREVER

• • • • •

Stay tuned for the next
snap-tastic Liv and Maddie book

DOUBLE TROUBLE

available summer 2015!